D0792101

There's an ELF IN YOUR BOOK

Written by TOM FLETCHER

Illustrated by GREG ABBOTT

Random House 🏠 New York

For Buzz, Buddy, and Max
—T.F.

For Annika
—G.A.

Copyright © 2019 by Tom Fletcher
Illustrated by Greg Abbott

All rights reserved. Published in the United States by
Random House Children's Books, a division of
Penguin Random House LLC, New York.
Originally published by Puffin Books,
an imprint of Penguin Random House Children's Books, U.K.,
a division of Penguin Random House, U.K., London, in 2019.

Random House and the colophon are registered
trademarks of Penguin Random House LLC.

Visit us on the Web! rhcbooks.com

Educators and librarians, for a variety of teaching tools,
visit us at RHTeachersLibrarians.com

Library of Congress Cataloging-in-Publication Data
Names: Fletcher, Tom, author. | Abbott, Greg, illustrator.
Title: There's an elf in your book / written by Tom Fletcher ;
illustrated by Greg Abbott.
Other titles: There is an elf in your book
Description: First American edition. | New York: Random House, [2019] |
Summary: Invites the reader to take the Nice List test, while avoiding mischievous
Elf's naughty tricks, to prove Santa should bring Christmas presents to him or her.
Identifiers: LCCN 2019008069 | ISBN 978-1-9848-9344-4 (trade hardcover) |
ISBN 978-1-9848-9345-1 (ebook)
Subjects: | CYAC: Questions and answers—Fiction. |
Behavior—Fiction. | Elves—Fiction. | Christmas—Fiction. | Humorous stories.
Classification: LCC PZ7.F6358 Thm 2019 | DDC [E]—dc23

MANUFACTURED IN CHINA
10 9 8 7 6 5 4 3 2 1
First American Edition

OH, LOOK!

There's an elf
in your book!

Elf's here to do the Nice List test with you.

(You need to be on the Nice List if you want
Santa to bring you Christmas presents!)

For you to pass the test, Elf will ask you to do some **NICE** things.

But **WATCH OUT!** Elves can be a bit mischievous!

Don't get tricked into being **NAUGHTY**, okay?

When you're ready to take the test,
turn the page.

Good luck!

Let's start with an easy one.

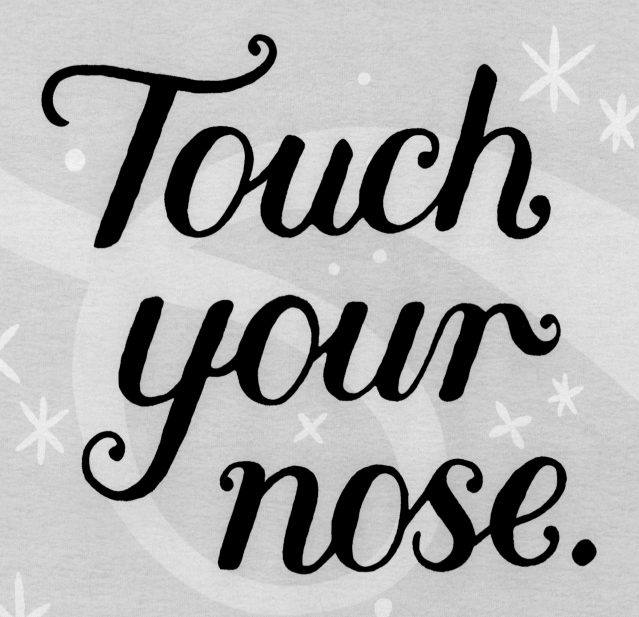

Touch your nose.

To see if you passed the test,
turn the page. . . .

Good job! You passed the first test.
Now . . .

Blow a Christmas kiss.

Do you think you passed?

What a lovely Christmas kiss!
You passed the second test. What's next?

Sing a cheery Christmas song.

Let's see if you passed. . . .

Beautiful singing!
You passed the third test. Now . . .

Say "I'm a wisenheimer sparkle butt!"

Wait a second—this sounds like a naughty trick!
I think Elf is testing you.

DON'T say "I'M A WISENHEIMER
SPARKLE BUTT!" Now turn the page. . . .

PHEW! It *was* a trick.
Thank goodness you didn't say it.
You passed the fourth test.

*How is the Nice List test
going so far, Elf?*

Awesome! Keep it up.

Name Santa's most famous reindeer.

RUDOLPH! Correct! You passed the fifth test. You're great at this. Now . . .

Do your loudest, stinkiest pizza burp!

EWWW!

STOP, STOP, STOP!

Do you think this is another naughty elf trick?

It *was* another trick—good catch!
Keep this up and you'll be on the Nice List in no time!

What's next, Elf?

Now for the final test . . .

Make Elf laugh.

Well, to make Elf laugh, you'll have to tell a joke.
Have a look in *The Christmas Joke Book*.

Turn the page to open it.

The CHRISTMAS JOKE BOOK

WHAT DO Elves DO IN THE TOILET?

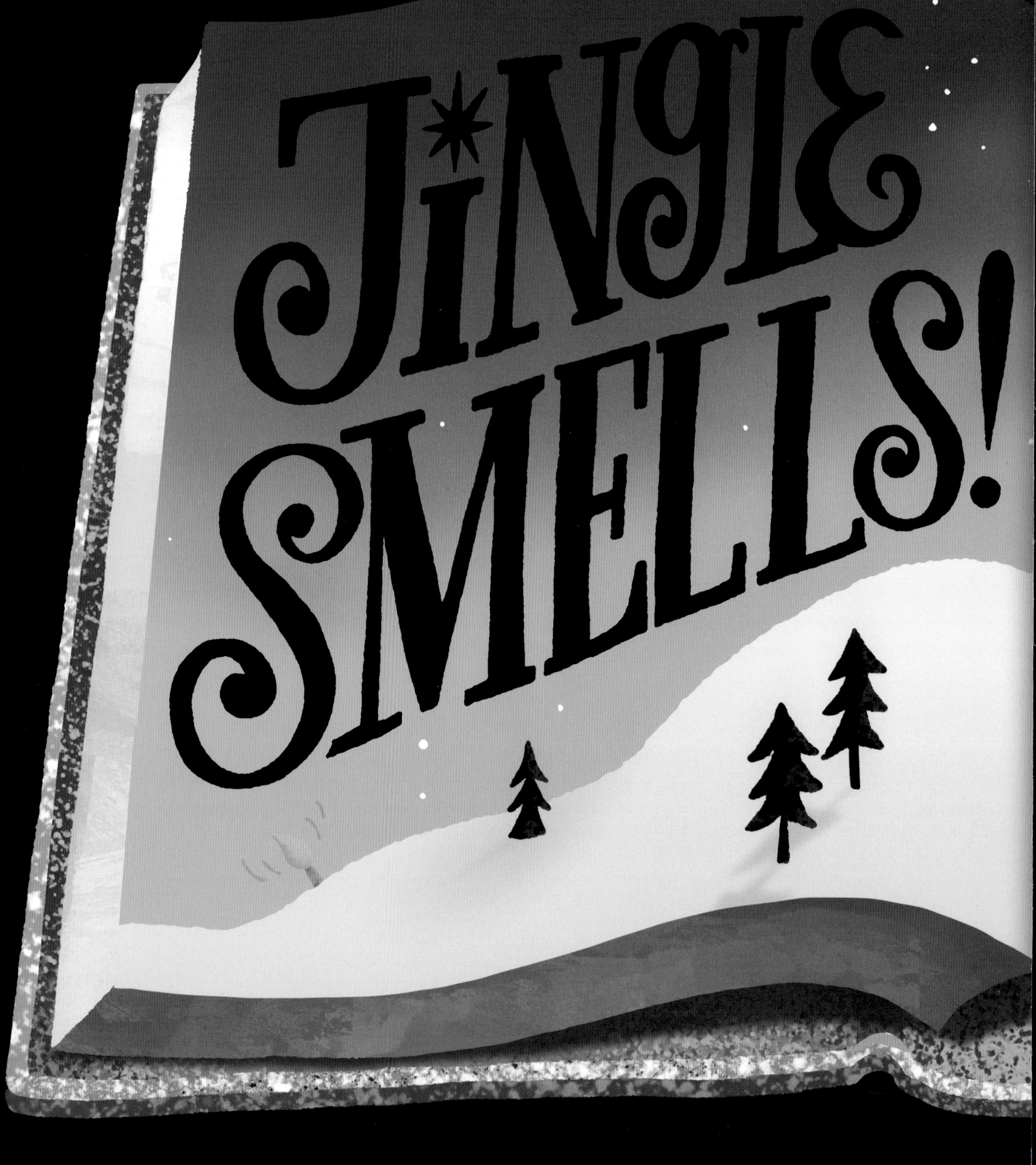
JINGLE
SMELLS!

Oh No!

The joke was a mischievous elf trick
to make you say something naughty!

Does this mean you
failed the test?

Surely you can't be on the Nice List
if you've done something naughty.

It looks as though Elf feels bad
for tricking you, but rules are rules. . . .

Hang on a second!
The test was to make Elf laugh,
and **YOU DID**, so . . .

You passed
the
Nice List
test!

Hurray!
You are officially on the Nice List.

And look—what's this?

WOW, it's your

OFFICIAL

NICE LIST

·◆· CERTIFICATE ·◆·

Make sure you leave this book out
on Christmas Eve—Santa will
want to check it.

Until then, Merry Christmas!
STAY NICE!

BY Elf